# Horse On The Loose

Leslie McDonald

Monday Creek Publishing
Ohio USA

# Copyright



# Illustrator

Cover art and interior illustrations by Tanya Glebova. Ms. Glebova is from Kharkov, Ukraine. She teaches drawing and sculpture at the local University. She loves to draw and for the last four years she has been creating book illustrations, where she is in her "element" - drawing pets, traditional styles, and modern digital art.

# Book Reviews

As an author, I highly appreciate the feedback I get from my readers. It helps others to make an informed decision when buying my books. If you enjoyed this book, please consider leaving a short review on amazon. Thank you.

# Dedication

To all the special senior horses who loyally help their human partners to reach for the stars and achieve their dreams. They fulfill us through their generosity, patience, dedication and love.

A heartfelt thanks to some of the wonderful senior horses who have blessed my life and provided inspiration for this story, including Tic-Tac, Borne, Anders, Anastasia, Rasir, Dauntless  and, of course, Quin.

# Other Titles From Leslie McDonald

Visit Leslie's Amazon Author Page

*Down the Aisle*
*Musings of a Horse Farm Corgi*
*Journeys with Horses*
*Making Magic*
*Tic-Tac*

# Table of Contents

# Chapter One
# The Great Escape

The faded bay horse waited patiently in his stall at the end of the barn aisle. His once sleek mahogany coat was beginning to gray. White hairs fanned out from the top of his wide blaze to the corner of his eyes. The muscles of his top line had relaxed into the soft, overweight curves of a comfortable retirement.

For 10 years a brass nameplate that read "Mighty Quin owned by Dawn Miller" had hung on his stall door. It was a fitting name for the horse who had been a great jumper champion in his day. Quin was happy the day Dawn had come into his life when she was just eight. He was a winning schoolmaster, purchased by her parents to give her confidence and experience. From their first ride together, he loved how she always called him her "forever friend."

Season after season he had been proud to carry Dawn around courses on the big show circuit to win countless blue ribbons and trophies. Ever dependable, he never missed a distance or took down a rail. But eventually time and age caught up with him, making the courses seem a little too long and the fences a little too high. Loving and respecting her partner, Dawn retired him from competition while he was still a champion.

At first Quin missed the fast paced thrill and glory of the show ring. He had been uncertain about the change in routine brought about by retirement. However, it didn't take him long to forget the hard daily workouts required to keep competition fit when those training sessions were replaced by long, leisurely trail rides.

He happily carried Dawn through the meadows and woods beyond the stable. Their favorite resting spot was a big oak tree that stood alone in the center of a distant field. Dawn would hop off to sit cross legged in the shade of the tree beside Quin while he grazed and nibbled carrot treats from her pocket. Rested and snack finished, they would be off again to explore new horizons until the sun set.

But the picnic rides had abruptly ended a month ago. On that day, Dawn arrived at the stable dressed in grey slacks and a pale blue sweater instead of her usual boots and breeches. Quin was concerned; sensing an unusual sadness as she slowly stroked his neck. "No riding today, Quin. I have to leave for college."

She gave a long sniff, wiping away a tear. "I wish I didn't have to go, but I promise it won't be forever. You won't be lonesome. Andy will turn you out every day to run in the pasture with your buddies. And, I'll be home for vacations, so we can go for our rides again. But, I sure am going to miss you."

Dawn hugged his neck tightly for a very long time. When she finally let go, he was surprised to feel his coat was wet from her tears. Filling his feed box with apples and his favorite molasses treats, she quickly left the stall.

Puzzled, Quin watched her walk away. Her sadness was contagious. He didn't understand what college was or why it was taking her away from him. "Don't go, Dawn!" he whinnied loudly and pawed the stall door, demanding her return. But in response, she hurried out of the stable unable to look back.

All that morning he remained at his Dutch door, neck stretched out to see to the end of the aisle. He stared intently at the entrance, willing Dawn to return, but she never did. Not that day or the next or even the following week. But still he waited, unable to believe that his "forever friend" had deserted him.

*Every day from his stall, Quin faithfully watched for Dawn's return. He refused to give up on his "forever friend."*

The lonely days dragged on without any sign of Dawn. Quin couldn't stop from wondering what had become of her. The thought of his partner never returning frightened him. *What if she doesn't want me just because I can't win in the show ring anymore?*

Even though his groom, Andy, brushed his coat to a shine every morning and turned him out to graze with the other horses, it wasn't the same without Dawn. No one else's hand could replace the special way she ran her fingers along his neck, pulling gently on his mane.

During those long, empty days without Dawn, he started thinking about an old horse he had known named Admiral. They had been stablemates when Quin was a youngster at his first training barn. As Quin was on his way up the competition ladder, Admiral was on the way down from his pinnacle as a champion show hunter. For years, Admiral had performed his heart out for his rider until it became too hard to jump the big fences with the style the judges demanded. When he could no longer win, his owner sold him to a riding school, replacing him with a flashy new youngster ready to make his mark in the show ring.

The rumor among the stable horses was that instead of receiving a well-earned retirement, Admiral had spent his final years giving endless riding lessons to beginners. His stablemates agreed that teaching was an admirable profession. However, they also felt that at the end of a winning career, a champion like Admiral deserved to retire from work to be spoiled and loved by the person for whom he had won so many victories.

Quin angrily stomped his hoof at the thought of Admiral's unfair fate. He was determined not to let the same thing happen to him. *If Dawn doesn't love me enough to share my senior years as she shared the rewards of my youth, I'll find a new home. It will be a special place where people appreciate me for who I am, not just for what I can win for them.*

His mind made up, Quin resolved to set a plan in action before the humans in his life made choices for his future that he didn't want.

He was ready the next morning when Andy pushed a big wheelbarrow filled with breakfast hay down the aisle. The groom gave all the horses a cheery greeting as they impatiently pawed and snorted to be fed. "Mornin' my pretties. Hope you all slept well. Patience now. Quit your banging. There's plenty of hay for everyone."

Quin joined in the clamor to be fed, his voice blending in with the whinnies and stomps of the other horses demanding breakfast. Although he pretended be part of the hungry morning chorus, Quin vowed that today would be different. Instead of accepting a sad fate like Admiral's, this day he would take control of his own destiny.

Andy finally stopped the wheelbarrow in front of Quin's stall. "Quiet down, old man. You may be the senior horse in this barn, but you still raise a ruckus like a colt at feeding time."

Quin impatiently shook his thick black mane. "Old man!" he scoffed with an insulted snort for he wasn't thinking of filling his stomach, but of the moment the groom would slide open the door. *Just wait a bit and I'll show you that this old man has still got it!* Quin vowed as he waited for his chance.

Quin nickered a soft welcome in the back of his throat as Andy opened the door latch. "Here you go, old man," he said giving him a friendly pat on the neck. "You're a noisy one this morning."

As Andy stepped in to toss the hay into the manger, Quin saw his opportunity. Shoving his shoulder between the groom and the door, he bolted out of the stall. Andy made a desperate grab for his halter, but it was too late. Quin was out the door ahead of him, sparks jumping off the aisle floor as his hooves slid across the concrete.

"Whoa, Quin, whoa!" Andy cried, running after him. "Where are you going? Come back!"

But his shouts only made Quin run faster. With a defiant toss of his head, he galloped out the open aisle door toward the path that led to freedom in the fields beyond the stable.

"I'm free! From now on, I'm the one who gets to decide my future," Quin rejoiced with a loud whinny as he charged out of the barn.

Andy waved frantically at two girls who were riding in the outdoor arena. "Quin's loose! Cut him off before he gets off the property!"

Hearing the urgency in his voice, the girls quickly turned their horses in the direction that Andy was pointing toward. Cantering quickly out of the arena, they cut Quin off just before he reached the path that led away from the stable.

"Whoa, Quin! Easy boy!" the girls cried, reining their horses as close as possible to prevent him from escaping.

Penned in, Quin slid to a stop, spinning back toward the barn. The girls were quick to pivot their horses, taking up the chase. Galloping alongside, one of the girls leaned far out of her saddle reaching for his halter. She made a grab, but Quin was too quick. He bucked and kicked out as her hand came within inches of his cheek piece.

Arms waving, Andy ran toward him. "Whoa, Quin! What are you doing? Stop, old man!"

"Old man?!" Quin angrily snorted as he spun away, his hooves defiantly spraying driveway gravel in Andy's direction. "Just try and stop me!"

In response to Andy's shouts, other grooms began running from the barn to help. Seeing people rushing toward him from all directions, Quin knew he had to think fast before he was trapped and captured. There was no way he was going to let them take away his hard-earned freedom.

The brick stable wall prevented escape to the left. On his right, the two girls on horseback closed in fast. Behind him, Andy and his posse of barn workers tightened the circle. The only possible escape was straight ahead over a five-foot-tall board fence that separated the stable grounds from the neighboring golf course.

Quin had never set a hoof on the lush green fairway grass that ran alongside the stable property. All the riders knew their horses were forbidden to trespass. Avoiding temptation, Dawn and her friends were careful to keep them far away from the bordering fence knowing the country club imposed steep fines for any horse that strayed onto the golf course.

Quin gave the fence a long, doubtful look. It had been years since he cleared such a high fence. Even at the peak of his career, that height had been a stretch for him. He remembered his last competition feeling the top rail rub his belly as he tucked his knees up to his nose to jump clear. But, as his pursuers closed in, he didn't dare hesitate if he was to gain his freedom.

Lengthening his strides, he sped up, heading straight for the fence. *My future is on the other side of that fence.*

*There's no other way. I have to clear it!* Quin resolved as he galloped forward.

"NO, QUIN, NO!" Andy cried in desperation. "DON'T JUMP!"

"WHOA!" the girls screamed, pulling up their horses. "STOP!"

But their pleas only made Quin more determined. *I have to clear the fence. It's the most important jump of my life*, he thought as he galloped faster toward the base, eyeing the perfect take off point.

With a final deep breath, he jumped high and wide, pushing his muscles harder than he had in years. Pure determination catapulted him over the boards with room to spare. Landing easily on the soft grass on the far side, he was away with a cocky flip of his tail, never looking back at the stable or his pursuers.

"*Whoo hoo!"* Quin whinnied loudly as he galloped to freedom across the beautiful green golf course. *"I did it!"*

*Determined to escape the stable and his uncertain future, Quin gave a maximum effort to soar over the big rail fence to freedom.*

# Chapter Two
# Fairway to Freedom

Quin's shoes dug into the golf course turf as he raced away from the fence. Big chunks of rich sod flew through the air in his wake. He loved the spongy feel of the thick grass beneath his hooves.

Behind him, the girls were forced to pull up their horses in front of the fence. Knowing the fines per hoof print the country club would enforce on horses trespassing, they didn't dare risk following Quin over the big jump. However, Andy and the other grooms had no such worries since they followed on foot. They quickly scrambled over the rails to keep up the chase.

Celebrating his freedom, Quin joyfully shook back his mane. He galloped down the fairway, thrilled with the success of his escape plan. From now on “nobody’s going to decide my future but me!” he rejoiced with a loud, triumphant whinny.

Quin didn’t slow down until he could no longer hear Andy shouting for him to stop. When he finally looked over his shoulder, he was pleased to see that the groom and his posse had turned around and were running back toward the stable. He came to a walk with a satisfied snort to catch his breath.

Feeling safe at last, he gave into the temptation to explore the golf course. Although he knew it was off limits to horses, the rolling green turf had always been a temptation to Quin and his stablemates. They dreamed of burying their muzzles into the rich grass to fill their bellies with what they were certain was far tastier food than their daily stable fare.

Not far ahead, a banked depression filled with white sand caught his eye. Curious, he trotted over to investigate. Tentatively, he extended a front leg over the rim. He pawed at the sand that looked similar to the footing in the stable’s riding arena. Stretching his neck down, he took a deep sniff.

“Whuff!” he sneezed as the fine grains tickled his nose.

Quin carefully stepped over the edge of the sand trap. He pawed a deep hole in the middle then dropped to his knees with a contented sigh. Flopping over onto his side in the cool sand, he kicked his hooves high in the air, enjoying the perfect back scratch.

He rolled and rolled and rolled until he was almost dizzy with joy. “This is fun! I like being in charge,” Quin whinnied loudly.

When every inch of his back and neck had been itched, he stood up to shake the sand out of his coat. Only then did he notice three red golf carts in the distance, speeding in his direction. Looking closer, he recognized Andy leading the charge in the front cart.

Without wasting another moment, Quin scrambled out of the sand trap. *I'd better get out of here and fast*, he thought, galloping away toward an oval shaped putting green at the far end of the fairway.

A foursome of golfers stood on the green preparing to putt. Deeply focused on their game, they were unaware of Quin's approach followed closely by the three golf carts. In the forefront of the group, a golfer in a white shirt and bright red pants bent over his ball. Concentrating on the shot, he lined the ball up with the hole that was just three feet away.

“Relax, relax,” the golfer coached himself, making a final tiny adjustment to his putter. “Just a few easy feet and it's in for a birdie. Just three feet and I win the round.”

Slowly he drew back the putter, holding his breath to steady his hands to make the perfect shot. But, just at that moment, Quin bolted onto the green from behind.

“Chuck, watch out!” one of the other men shouted. “Loose horse!”

Startled, Chuck spun around. His carefully aimed putter smashed into the ball, sending it over the hole to bury in the sand trap on the far side of the green. Frightened to see Quin only strides away, he dove into the sand trap after his ball just in time to avoid being run over by churning hooves.

“Stupid horse!” Chuck yelled, shaking his putter at Quin from the safety of the sand trap. “You ruined my game! How did that horse get onto the golf course?”

Frightened by their shouts, Quin galloped even faster. He sped past Chuck and the other golfer who threatened him from the safety of the sand trap.

*Why is everyone so mad?* Quin wondered, putting as much distance as possible between himself, the golfers and Andy’s carts that were still in hot pursuit.

He cantered beyond the fairway onto a large expanse of longer grass marked at different intervals by poles with flapping red flags. Suddenly, without warning, a golf ball hit him sharply in the flank.

“Ow!” Quin snorted when a second ball popped into his shoulder and then another against his neck. He shied to the left then to the right, but no matter which way he turned, balls kept whizzing toward him.

*Quin couldn't understand why the golfers were so mad as he galloped across the golf course churning up big chunks of turf with his hooves.*

"Fore!" a voice shouted.

Quin wheeled around to see three men standing in a line at the edge of the field. They all swung golf clubs, hitting balls in his direction.

"Get that horse off the driving range!" one of them yelled.

Quin didn't need a third warning. He galloped away, not stopping until he was far out of the target zone. Looking back, he was relieved to see that Andy and his golf cart posse had detoured around the range rather than follow him across.

Directly ahead stood a big, brick clubhouse surrounded by tall shade trees. Curious, Quin trotted forward, stopping behind a hedge that surrounded the manicured grounds. He nibbled a hole through the branches to check out what was on the other side.

In front of him was a large courtyard with a fountain in the middle of a round fish pond. People sat in wrought iron chairs beneath green and white striped umbrella tables as waiters in white jackets served them breakfast. Quin tilted his head, fascinated to see how humans were fed their meals so unlike horses.

But his curiosity was quickly distracted by the renewed sound of sputtering golf carts. Sensing Andy and his posse closing in again, he looked for the quickest escape route. The best option was directly ahead. Without hesitation, he bolted around the end of the hedge and across the breakfast courtyard.

Startled by the sudden appearance of a big, charging brown horse, people panicked and jumped to their feet. Frightened by their screams, Quin galloped across the concrete, overturning tables and chairs in his wake.

A waiter waved his arms to divert him, but try as Quin might to avoid a collision, his shoulder knocked the man aside as he rushed past. “Sorry!” Quin whinnied as he sped on. “I didn’t mean it!”

Directly in Quin’s path, another waiter carefully carried a full tray of breakfast dishes. Balancing his load until the last moment, the man stumbled to the ground as he dove out of Quin’s way. As he fell, dishes, food and glasses flew in all directions, shattering on the ground. “Really sorry!” Quin nickered apologetically.

In close pursuit, Andy and his golf cart posse sped around the hedge and into the courtyard. Hoping to cut Quin off, the first driver took a corner too tight, catching the edge of the fish pond. The front tire jammed against the concrete, overturning the cart and throwing the two occupants head first into the water.

Their accident gave Quin just enough time to escape the terrace. In a flash he was off, speeding across the parking lot toward the tennis court where two couples were

*Quin tried to apologize as he knocked over a waiter on his dash to escape across the country club breakfast patio.*

playing doubles. The players were so intent on their game that they didn't notice him until he was nearly at the edge of their court.

"George!" one of the women screeched. "Loose horse!" first into the water.

The others looked up just as Quin dashed across the court. His hooves dug up the smooth clay surface, cutting through the white boundary lines.

"Stop him!" the other woman yelled. "He's ruining the court!"

"Catch him, George!" her partner shouted across the net. "He's on your side."

"Excuse me. Just passing through," Quin whinnied as he galloped across the court.

George ran toward Quin, swinging his racket to stop him. But Quin swerved, jumping easily over the net far out of the man's reach.

"E-e-e-h!" the woman in his path screamed, scurrying to get out of the way of his hooves.

*I don't understand,* Quin worried, alarmed by the yelling. *Everyone at home always liked me, but all the people here seem so angry with me.*

Charging away, Quin quickly left the players and their trampled tennis court in his wake. He galloped on through a rose garden that separated the country club from the road.

Jumping a hedge of pink flowers, he found himself on a road leading away from the club.

Quin continued his flight down the shoulder of the road, not slowing down until the clubhouse and the golf carts were far behind. Out of breath and energy, he noticed a cluster of trees and slipped between them. He worked his way deep into the foliage to keep out of sight of anyone passing on the road.

Exhausted, Quin listened carefully for the return of Andy's golf cart posse. But surrounded only by the comforting chirps of birds and the rustling leaves of the trees, he finally began to feel safe.

He nibbled at the thin grass under foot, pondering his newfound freedom. In the past, he had always relied on Dawn's steady confidence to guide him through new experiences. However, without her by his side, the escape had been far more challenging than he had ever imagined when planning it from the safety of his stall.

*It'll be okay,* Quin reassured himself. *I'll figure all this out. Even if Dawn doesn't want me anymore, I'll be just fine because I'm in charge now.*

Quin sighed with exhaustion. For now, he was too tired to worry about his next move. Dropping down to the ground, he laid his head on a pile of damp leaves and quickly fell into a deep sleep.

# Chapter Three
# The Quest Begins

Quin was awakened by a loud chirp. He lifted his head from the ground with a start, trying to remember where he was. Shaking his forelock, he knocked off a tiny sparrow that had been perched comfortably between his ears. The little bird flew up to a nearby branch, angrily scolding Quin for disrupting his nap.

"H-u-m-p-h!" Quin snorted back at him. "I am NOT a bed!"

The sparrow curiously cocked his head. "What are you doing in my forest?" he chirped down from his branch.

Quin sighed. "I'm a champion show horse who used to live nearby in a stable. For many years, I had a wonderful owner who shared my life. I thought she loved me, but she's stopped coming to see me."

"Why would she do that if she loves you?" the sparrow asked.

Quin looked sadly up at the little bird. "I think because I've grown too old to do the job she expects of me. I'm afraid I'll be sold and replaced by a younger horse that can win ribbons for her at the shows."

Feeling sorry for Quin, the sparrow fluttered down to perch on his shoulder. "That's just not right. But, what can you do?"

Grateful for his sympathy, Quin bent his neck around to gently nuzzle the little bird. "Yesterday I ran away from home before they could sell me. I'm taking control of my destiny to find the perfect home where people want me for who I am."

The sparrow gave Quin's nose a understanding peck. "Best of luck, friend. I hope you find what you're looking for."

As the sparrow flew off into the trees, Quin slowly rolled to his feet, stretching aching muscles. His sore body reminded him it had been a long time since he had run and jumped that hard. Living the life of a retired show horse had definitely not kept him conditioned for a golf course run.

Hungry, he sniffed the ground for breakfast, but there was no fresh hay or sweet oats to fill his grumbling belly. Underfoot, he found only bitter weeds and thin grass.

He was stiff from sleeping on the hard ground instead of his stall's soft bed of shavings that Andy never failed to fluff deep. For 10 years it had been his home. From the very first day, he loved his stall and his stablemate. The board wall that separated them bore hoof kick impressions from their arguments at feeding time. But, it had never been more than friendly bickering between two buddies; a buddy he missed very much right now.

And then there was his Dutch door. It had allowed him to stretch his neck out into the aisle to be admired and patted by passersby. He also missed Andy's special care. The groom could always be counted on to have a tasty sugar treat in his pocket and a special massaging touch to ease sore muscles.

But, most of all, he missed Dawn. For years, she had been his special person making certain he received the best of care. In return, he never let her down no matter how high she asked him to jump or how fast she wanted to gallop. After all they had shared, he couldn't understand how she could abandon him just because he had grown old. He shook his head sadly realizing it was only a matter of time before his well-earned retirement would be snatched away from him, just like it had been for his friend Admiral.

*Why do things have to change?* Quin wondered. *I still have a lot to give Dawn. But, since I haven't seen her for weeks, it seems that she's done with me. There's nothing more to do but move on and find a new home where I'm wanted; a home that I can pick this time.*

His mind made up, he walked to the edge of the trees and poked out his head, checking for signs of Andy and his golf cart posse. A long look left then right assured him the coast was clear. Feeling safe, he stepped out into the sunlight and turned down the road in a new direction. Quin had no idea where he was headed, but he was certain that somewhere along the route he would find the perfect new home.

*I know there's a place where people will love and appreciate me,* Quin resolved as he started off on his quest. *I'm going to find it no matter how long it takes or how far I have to travel.*

Feeling confident, he trotted along the grassy boulevard, passing long driveways that led to big houses set behind high hedges. There were very few cars on the road, but whenever one passed, Quin veered as close as possible toward the safety of the hedges. Although some slowed down, none tried to pursue him.

He didn't worry until a dark blue car pulled alongside. It changed speed to keep pace with his strides. A small, red faced boy wearing a baseball cap leaned so far out of the window that his mother had to grab his belt to keep him from tumbling out.

"Here, horse! Here!" the boy cried, excitedly waving his cap at Quin. "Catch him, Mommy! Catch him! I want to ride the horse!"

Certain that the child was not the person he was searching for, Quin quickened his stride and galloped down the nearest driveway. The car paused at the entrance, but to Quin's relief, it did not follow him. He waited behind the hedge until he was certain the car with the loud little boy was gone.

Trotting back out onto the road, he continued on his way. The wide boulevard began to narrow until there was nothing left underfoot but a concrete sidewalk. The big houses fronted by wide grass yards were gradually replaced by shops and offices. The closer he came to the town center the more crowded the street became with traffic and honking cars.

Quin's ears twitched back and forth. The strange city noises made him nervous. There were loud whistles and the squeal of tires as well as shouts and clanks that he had never heard in the safety of his stable. He kept close to the store fronts, trying not to attract attention.

Suddenly, a door slammed close behind. Startled, Quin spun around only to find himself face to face with his own reflection in the glass of a store window. Never before having seen his reflection, he was certain he had come upon another horse.

Overjoyed at finding a kindred spirit in the busy town, he nickered a welcome. “Hey, buddy, am I glad to see you!”

When there was no response from the bay horse who stared back at him from the window, Quin stretched out his neck to touch noses. But, to his surprise, instead of touching a soft muzzle, his nose hit cold, hard glass.

Just then a woman screamed from across the street. “HORSE! Help! Police! Loose horse!”

Her terrified shouts brought people running from all directions. They came out of stores, down the sidewalk and even stopped their cars in the middle of the street to discover the cause of her screams.

“Look, Sherry! There’s a horse on the sidewalk!” an elderly woman who was out shopping with her granddaughter pointed.

“Where did he come from?” the little girl exclaimed.

“Somebody catch him!” a man in a blue car shouted as he drove by.

“Careful. He might be dangerous!” a young mother with a baby worried, pulling her child closer to her.

One of the shop owners tried to calm the crowd. “Wait for the police. They’ll know what to do.”

Quin quickly backed down the sidewalk away from the

scary noises and gathering crowd. He was so focused on escaping that he never noticed a woman overloaded with grocery bags coming out of the store behind him. Before she could cry out, his rump bumped into her chest. Cans, bottles and boxes flew into the air as she fell over backwards onto the pavement.

"Ahhhhh!" she cried, rolling over to get out of his way. "Help! Help!"

Startled by her screams, Quin quickly bolted forward. "I'm really sorry," he nickered over his shoulder as he hurried away.

People who were just as frightened of him as he was of them waved their arms as he passed, but no one was bold enough to make a grab for his halter. They scattered as he surged between them to gallop off the sidewalk and down the center of the street.

Cars slammed on their brakes to avoid hitting him as he zig zagged across the lanes of traffic. The driver of a red SUV smashed into the fender of the van in front of him that swerved around Quin at the last minute. The van's sudden turn caused the convertible in the next lane to crash into his bumper. Soon even more horns were blaring, adding to the commotion. Drivers jumped out of their cars, shouting and shaking fists at each other and at Quin.

"Stop that horse!" an angry driver yelled.

"Look at my car! It's ruined!" the SUV driver exclaimed.

"Where's that horse's owner? I want to talk to that guy!" another driver stuck in the traffic jam shouted out of his window.

Terrified by the growing noise and seeing no escape through the traffic that blocked the road in both directions, Quin stopped suddenly in the middle of the busy intersection. *Why are they so angry?* he wondered, searching for a way out. *I've always felt safe with humans, but these people look like they want to hurt me!*

As the crowd closed in, for the first time in his life, Quin felt the need to defend himself. Rearing high in the air, he struck out with his front hooves to warn the people to stay away.

"T-w-e-e-t … t-w-e-e-t … t-w-e-e-t!" A shrill whistle sounded above the commotion as four uniformed policemen ran down the street toward Quin.

"Whoa, horse, whoa!" the lead officer shouted. "Steady, boy!"

"Get behind him, Frank!" the second officer directed the man in the lead.

"I'll get the left side, you take the right," the third officer offered.

"All set?" the officer bringing up the rear asked when they had formed a small circle around Quin who continued to rear in his defense. “One, two, three, grab him!”

On the final count, they lunged awkwardly forward. It only took Quin a moment to recognize that while they might be confident taking down crooks, they had no horse handling sense. Taking advantage of their inexperience, he jumped sideways, knocking the closest officer to the pavement with his shoulder.

“Sorry, buddy,” Quin whinnied as he took flight, tripping the next officer who tried to grab for his halter.

The downed officers were quick to jump to their feet. They ran for their squad cars to take up the chase. But to their dismay, they found them blocked by the traffic jam that had grown around Quin. They were left with no option, but to radio headquarters to dispatch new cars to pursue the runaway horse that with a flip of his tail had disappeared from sight.

As fast as his legs would carry him, Quin turned his back on the whistles, blaring car horns and angry shouts of the town. *There is definitely no place for a horse here!* he decided, making his getaway down a side street.

Even when the shops and officers were far behind, he didn’t slow down. He was on the run again, trying to put as much distance as possible between himself and the town where he was certain the perfect new home did not exist.

# Chapter Four
# An Unwelcome Hideaway

Big, black storm clouds rolled quickly across the sky, blocking out the midday sun as Quin cantered on. He was exhausted, but determined to get as far away as possible from the town where he had felt so unwelcome. Hoping to throw the police off his trail, he left the open roadway for the safety of the surrounding fields.

Lightning slashed the sky, followed by a loud clap of thunder. The wind whistled and gusted through his mane as he skirted a corn field behind a row of houses. Quin lifted his head and flared his nostrils. He could smell rain in the air. Storms always made him uneasy, so he knew it was time to find safe shelter before it broke.

He trotted cautiously toward a grey ranch house with a green storage shed in the backyard. The small metal building looked like it had possibilities for protection from the storm. Not seeing any people in the yard, he decided to investigate.

Quin approached very slowly, his ears twitching back and forth to pick up any threatening noises. He was ready to run away at the first sound of voices. But when he reached the shed without being noticed, he felt it was safe to explore. He gave the door handle a soft nudge with his nose. To his delight, it easily swung open.

It was hard to see inside. Without any windows, the only light that came into the shed was through the door he had just opened. Quin could make out an assortment of garden tools, hoses, buckets and baskets crowded into the little building. There was barely floor space for a dog let alone a big brown horse. But before he could turn to search for more suitable shelter, the first drops of rain splattered against his back followed by another loud clap of thunder.

*I'll have to be creative to make this work,* Quin decided, realizing he was out of time to find a better hideaway. He stuck his neck far into the shed, dragging out anything he could lift with his teeth. Soon there were rakes, shovels, grass seed bags and bushel baskets scattered outside across the lawn. But despite his best efforts, the little building was still very crowded.

Shaking the rain off his back, Quin studied the set up in the shed. *I think the best way in is backwards,* he determined.

Pushing in with his hindquarters, he wiggled into a cramped space in the center of the building. His hooves knocked against a stack of clay flower pots, breaking them into pieces. A straw basket hanging from the ceiling rested on his head. As the full fury of the storm hit, he grabbed the door handle between his teeth, pulling it closed just in time.

Standing with one hoof in a coiled garden horse and a basket resting on his head, Quin surveyed his current situation. *This is certainly not ideal, but at least I'm safe from the storm,* Quin thought gratefully.

As the storm crashed and howled around the shed, Quin fell into a restless sleep filled with nightmares of strangers chasing him and car horns honking. In his dreams, no matter which way he turned or how far he ran, big hands grabbed for his halter and mad voices shouted at him to stop.

Standing with one hoof in a coiled garden horse and a basket resting on his head, Quin surveyed his current situation. *This is certainly not ideal, but at least I'm safe from the storm,* Quin thought gratefully.

*Seeking shelter from the storm, Quin had to be creative to find a way to fit into the crowded toolshed.*

As the storm crashed and howled around the shed, Quin fell into a restless sleep filled with nightmares of strangers chasing him and car horns honking. In his dreams, no matter which way he turned or how far he ran, big hands grabbed for his halter and mad voices shouted at him to stop.

Quin didn't know how long he'd been asleep when he was suddenly awakened by an angry man's voice from outside the shed. Frightened, he threw up his head, but it was so dark in the little hideaway that he didn't know if it was day or night.

"Where did this mess come from?" the voice demanded. "I'll bet it was Joey and his friends again. Those kids know they're not allowed to play in my garden shed. Wait until I get hold of them. They're really in trouble this time!"

Quin nervously shuffled his hooves. *Uh oh, that sounds like trouble,* he worried, hoping the man would take his anger someplace else without looking inside the shed. But before Quin could think of an escape plan, the door swung open with a loud creak.

"What on earth!" a tall man exclaimed, his eyes wide with surprise. "A horse! Where did you come from? How on earth did you get in my shed?!"

Quin stared back just as startled. From the angry look on the man's face, he was certain this was not the home he was searching for. He struggled to free his hooves from the hose, ladder and potting soil where they had been planted all night. But, the man was too quick for Quin's stiff legs. He slammed the door tight before escape was possible.

"Take it easy, horse," the man ordered as he bolted the door shut. "I don't know how you got into my shed, but I'm going to find out where you came from. Maybe there's a reward for finding you."

*I've got to get out of here.* Quin frantically pawed the door of his shelter from the storm that had suddenly become a prison. He felt trapped without even a window to see outside. His hungry stomach gurgled without any hay or grain to eat. There wasn't even a bucket of water to quench his thirst.

It wasn't long before Quin heard the man returning. "That's right, Joey. There's a real live horse in our shed."

"Honest, Dad?" a young voice asked in awe.

"See for yourself," his father answered, sliding back the bolt to open the shed door a crack.

A small boy dressed in striped pajamas peered into the darkness. Quin stretched out his nose and nickered invitingly. "Give me a chance to show you how friendly I am and I know you'll let me out."

"Wow! He's neat Dad!" Joey exclaimed. "Can I keep him? Please? I always wanted a horse."

His father laughed. "I don't think so. We don't know anything about taking care of a horse. Besides, I'm sure he belongs to someone. I'll bet he just got lost and his owner is real worried. I'm going to call the police to see if they know anything about a loose horse."

"Can I pet him?' Joey asked hopefully.

"That's probably not a good idea," his father warned. "We don't have any experience with horses. This one might be dangerous."

Joey pointed to the nameplate on the halter. "Look Dad. His name is Mighty Quin. He sure seems friendly. You wouldn't hurt me, would you, Quin?"

Quin snorted and shook his head. He kept eye contact with the boy who he hoped would provide a way out of the shed.

"See, Dad, Quin understands!" Joey exclaimed with delight. "He's a smart horse. Now I'm sure he won't hurt me. Please let me pet him."

"I guess we could give it a try," his father relented. "But let me pet him first to make sure it's safe.

Quin pricked his ears, making his friendliest face to encourage them. He stood very still, waiting for the right moment. As Joey's father opened the door just far enough to reach inside, Quin attempted a surge toward freedom. But, with his hooves still tangled in the tools, he was too slow.

Before he could push through the opening, the man quickly pulled back his arm and slammed the door shut.

"He's a frisky one!" the man exclaimed with surprise. "Almost got away from us that time."

"Maybe we should let him out," Joey suggested. "We could tie him in the yard with a rope."

"I'm afraid we don't have a rope strong enough to hold a horse," his father answered. "No, we need to keep him in the shed until the police arrive. It's the safest place. Now let's go have breakfast while we wait for them. They'll know what to do."

"Please let me stay with Quin," Joey begged. "I'm not hungry. I'll bet he's lonely and wants company."

"Come on, son," his father directed. "I guarantee you the horse will still be here after we've eaten."

Feeling trapped in the little dark shed, Quin whinnied loudly. "Let me out! I won't hurt anyone. I just want to be free!"

He pawed hard at the door of his now unwelcome hideaway, trying to make Joey and his father understand that he was hungry and thirsty too. But, despite his protests, no one returned to let him out.

# Chapter Five
# A Fugitive from the Law

With the door closed and no windows to let in fresh air and light, the shed quickly grew hot and stuffy under the morning sun. Sweat broke out along Quin's neck and back. He continued to whinny and paw in protest, "Let me out! Let me out!" Still no one came to open the door.

When it seemed he couldn't bear the heat any longer, he finally heard Joey running back toward the shed. "Hurry, Dad! I want to see Quin again! Hurry!"

A moment later the bolt on the door slid back. "Take it easy horse," the man warned, carefully opening the door just enough to look inside.

"Can I feed him now?" Joey asked. "Please!"

Quin stopped pawing and pricked his ears at the

mention of food. *Please let it be alfalfa hay and apples,* he hoped.

"I'll be careful and pull my hand back real fast if he tries to bite just like you showed me, Dad," Joey promised. "But he looks like such a friendly horse, I'm sure he won't bite."

"Alright," his father finally agreed. "Remember to hold your hand flat. Keep your fingers tight together so he doesn't mistake them for food."

Quin nickered softly as Joey carefully stretched out his hand. *If he really does have food, I don't want to do anything to scare him.*

Joey laughed as Quin's chin whiskers tickled his hand. "Mom said horses like carrots and apples. I'm sorry we don't have any of those, but I brought you some radishes and a banana instead."

Quin curiously sniffed the small red vegetable, cautiously taking it from Joey's hand. *I have no idea what this is, but I'm so hungry I'll try anything,* he decided.

As soon as his teeth bit into the radish, he recoiled at the taste. Curling back his upper lip at the bitter flavor, he spit it back at Joey. No matter how his hungry belly grumbled for food, he was certain the radish was not the solution.

Joey offered a second radish, but to his disappointment Quin immediately turned his head away. "Guess he doesn't like it, Dad. Maybe he'd rather eat the banana."

The boy peeled the banana then offered it into the shed. Quin suspiciously sniffed the strong scent of the unfamiliar fruit. He definitely didn't like the soft, squishy feel beneath his nose. Taking a test bite, he spit it back at Joey just as quickly as the radish.

Quin was puzzled by the poor food options. *These people have absolutely no idea what horses like to eat. Andy never had a problem knowing what to feed me, but I can see that's going to be a serious consideration as I search for my new home.*

Joey was disappointed as he looked on the ground at his rejected food offerings. "I guess he's not hungry."

"I think you're right," his father agreed. "I'm sure the police will know what to do with him as soon as they get here."

At the mention of police, Quin's hunger disappeared. Based on his experience in town the previous day, he didn't want to have a second run in with the law. There was no choice but to escape from the shed before they arrived. He frantically pawed at the door, but Joey's father quickly bolted it shut again and left.

When Quin finally heard them return, they were followed by two new voices. "He's in that shed, officer," Joey's father explained. "You can imagine my surprise to find a horse there this morning. I have no idea how he got in."

*Quin curled up his nose at the radish. He was certain it wasn't horse food, but he was so hungry he was willing to give it a try.*

Quin was worried as he heard the bolt slide back and the shed door slowly open. He leaned back as far as possible waiting to see who was on the other side. A hand from a blue uniformed sleeve reached in toward him.

"Let's tie this rope to his halter and bring him out into the light for a good look," a voice at the end of the hand directed. "We had a call two days ago from a local stable about a runaway horse. Maybe this is him."

Quin tried to pull away from the hand, but the shed was too small to maneuver. He tossed his head, but the officer still managed to tie the rope to the halter ring.

"C'mon, horse," he gently urged, opening the door and tugging on the rope. "Cooperate with us. No one wants to hurt you."

Quin took an unsteady step. His legs were stiff and wobbly from standing all night in the tight space without moving. After so many hours in the dark shed, the bright sunlight momentarily blinded him. He blinked hard, trying to focus on the strangers in front of him.

"That's the horse that was loose in town yesterday!" the policeman holding the rope exclaimed the moment Quin walked out of the shed.

"Are you sure, Frank?" his partner asked.

"Believe me, after all we went through trying to catch this guy, I'll never forget him," Officer Frank vowed. "He caused a real commotion. Car wrecks everywhere. The townspeople are still cleaning up the mess."

Quin listened uneasily, wondering what they had planned for him. He remembered how angry the police had been when he'd escaped their trap in town. Hoping to pull free, he jerked up his head, but the officer held firm to the rope. Joey's eyes grew wide as he watched how skillfully the officer handled the rope. "What did Quin do?"

Officer Frank looked at him with surprise. "Did you call him Quin?"

Joey nodded. "That's his name. Mighty Quin. It's right there on his halter."

Officer Frank leaned forward to read the brass nameplate. "So it is. Well, that makes our job a lot easier. The horse that the stable lost is named Quin and his description fits this fellow. So it looks like we've found our lost horse."

He smiled, giving Quin a friendly pat on the neck. "Mystery solved, old boy. You've really wandered a long way from home, but we're going to see you get back where you belong safe and sound."

"I'll call the folks at the stable and tell them we've found their horse," his partner offered. "We'll have them drive right over with a trailer to pick him up. In the meantime, Mr. Grant, we'll need you to fill out some paperwork to close this case."

Joey's father ushered him toward the house. "Come sit down in the kitchen. We've got some coffee on."

Quin patiently watched the policeman follow Joey and his father into the house. He brightened, figuring his odds of escaping were definitely better with only one man to guard him.

Officer Frank stayed at his side, holding tight to the rope. He stroked Quin's bay neck as he nibbled grass in the back yard. "That's a good horse. Now don't cause us any more trouble. We'll get you back home with your people in no time."

Quin swished his tail and grazed, pretending to be the model of the perfectly obedient horse, waiting for the moment that the officer would relax his guard. *That's right. You can trust me. You don't have a thing to worry about,* Quin thought as he watched for his chance to escape.

As luck would have it, a few minutes later, a car backfired on the street in front of the house. The loud noise caused the officer to momentarily shift his attention. That was all the opportunity Quin needed to put his plan in action.

With a quick toss of his head, he tried to jerk the rope out of the man's hands. But, Officer Frank was quicker and stronger than Quin had guessed. Before he could pull the rope free, the man took a firmer grip.

"Sam, get out here!" he yelled, struggling to hang on. "I

need help. The horse is trying to get away!"

The louder his shouts, the harder Quin pulled. He reared high in the air, waving his hooves close to the policeman, careful not to hit him. He wanted to scare the man into letting go, but he didn't want to hurt him.

Officer Frank held up his left arm to protect his face from Quin's flailing hooves, but refused to let go of the rope with his right hand. "Whoa! Are you crazy horse? Whoa! What's gotten into you?"

In response to his shouts for help, Officer Sam and Mr. Grant came running from the house with Joey close behind. "Help me get him back in the shed or we're going to lose him again," Officer Frank directed. "He was grazing nice and quiet, but then a car backfired and he went nuts."

Joey's father and Officer Sam got behind Quin, waving their arms to try to shoo him back into the shed, but Quin refused to be herded. Bucking and pulling, he fought hard for his freedom. He didn't want to harm anyone, but he was determined not to be forced back into the dark, hot shed where there was no hope of escape.

When Officer Frank edged a little too close, Quin saw his chance. *Sorry, but you left me no choice,* he thought with a final rear that landed directly on the officer's right foot. *No one's taking me back to that stable to be sold. I'm in charge now and I plan to keep it that way!*

*Finally free of the shed and alone with the officer, Quin saw his chance and reared to escape the man's grasp.*

“Y-e-o-w!” Officer Frank screamed in pain, immediately dropping the rope to grab for his foot. “That big ox landed on my toes!”

Seeing his chance to escape, Quin bolted off across the field. The long rope dangled dangerously from his halter. It twisted between his legs as he galloped. He wanted to stop to chew it off, but there wasn’t time. He knew he had to put as much distance as possible between himself and the police. With a toss of his head, he untangled the rope from his legs and ran faster, celebrating his hard earned freedom. Once again he was on the loose and a fugitive from the law.

# Chapter Six
# Meet the Neighbors

Quin galloped hard for several miles without knowing where he was headed. His only goal was to put as much distance as possible between himself and the police. When he finally came to a forest, he ducked between the trees to hide himself in the deepest part.

He pushed far back through the underbrush searching for a safe place where he was certain no one passing on the road could see him. One fearful moment he heard loud sirens coming in his direction, but they passed his location without slowing. For the first time that day he finally felt safe.

His next concern was to get rid of the long rope that still dangled from his halter. Putting his right front hoof on the end of the rope to stabilize it, he set his teeth to work on the thick cotton strap. After an hour of tough chewing, he finally gnawed it off with a foot to spare from the end of his halter.

Exhausted, Quin settled down on the ground for a third lonely night. He had covered so many miles and seen so many new sights, but not one person except Joey had welcomed him. As he fell asleep, he wondered if his search would ever lead him to the ideal home.

Morning dawned clear and warm. A light breeze rustled the leaves of the trees. Sun streamed down through the branches. The woods came alive with birds, squirrels and rabbits searching for breakfast. He was awakened by a chipmunk scurrying over his hind ankles.

Quin stretched full out with a big yawn. The fresh morning air filled him with new hope. *I'm sure this is the day that I'll find the perfect home,* he assured himself.

Without wasting a moment more, he scrambled to his feet and trotted out of the woods to continue the search. To his right was a large corn field backed by another wooded area. On the left side of the road was a subdivision with neat rows of homes. Each house was surrounded by a large, shady yard with plenty of grass for a horse to eat.

Quin hesitated before starting forward. Although it looked peaceful, he was worried that the neighbors might be people like Joey's father who would lock him in a shed and only feed him radishes and bananas.

But he quickly shook off the thought with a toss of his mane. *I need to stay positive. With so many homes to choose from, there must be at least one family who would like to share their life with me.*

Recent experience had taught him the safest plan was to explore the area before making introductions to any of the people. He edged along the back of the properties, sampling mouthfuls of grass to see which was the sweetest. Even though several yards passed his taste test, Quin had learned there was more to finding the perfect owner than the quality of their grass. The time had come to meet the neighbors.

His first target was a grey brick house with a large picture window overlooking the back yard. There were two people in the kitchen, but Quin was too far away to see what they looked like. Gathering his courage, he walked up to the window and peered inside.

A man and his wife sat at the kitchen table eating breakfast and reading the newspaper. Neither of them noticed Quin until the woman got up to refill her coffee cup.

"E-e-e-h!" she screamed, dropping the cup on the floor when she saw Quin's big nose pressed against the window. "Chuck! A horse! There's a horse in our yard!"

Her husband turned in disbelief until he saw Quin. "It is a horse! Where did he come from?"

The woman backed quickly away from the window as though frightened that Quin might break through it. “I don’t care where he came from. Just get rid of him. I’m scared of horses! They’re so big!”

“Okay, okay,” her husband tried to calm her as she cowered behind him. “I’ll take care of him.”

He opened the back door and waved his arms toward Quin. “Get away, horse. Go on, shoo!”

But Quin held his ground. He responded with a soft nicker to convince them he was friendly and meant no harm.

“I said get away,” the man repeated, grabbing a roll of paper towels from the kitchen counter.

When Quin still refused to move, the man threw the towels, hitting him on the shoulder. That was all the warning Quin needed. He quickly spun and galloped off across the yard before the man could throw anything else.

Quin didn’t slow to a walk until the grey brick house was far out of sight, but he refused to be discouraged by this first defeat of the day. *Just because they didn’t want me, it doesn’t mean the people in the next house won’t,* he thought, determined to maintain a positive attitude.

Just ahead he noticed a stream of water shooting out of a lawn sprinkler. Feeling very thirsty, Quin trotted into the cool spray. He put his mouth close to the sprinkler. Curling back his lips, he let the water bubble into his mouth until he had drunk his fill.

Thirst quenched, he continued his search with new energy. In the next yard, he saw a clothesline hung with clean white sheets. His bay coat still dripping wet from the sprinkler spray, Quin trotted over to investigate. *This looks like fun!* he thought, rubbing his nose against the soft cotton fabric.

Giving it a sniff to be sure it was safe, he took the corner of one of the sheets between his teeth and tugged it off the line. Laying down on it with a sigh, he rolled over and over to dry himself. When the sheet was soaked from his wet coat, he stood up and pulled the next one off the line, enjoying the game. By the time his coat was finally dry, there were four grass stained sheets in a soiled pile on the ground.

As Quin pawed playfully at the dirty sheets, an angry woman hurried out of the house. “Oh, no!” she wailed. “Stupid horse! Look what you’ve done to my clean laundry!”

Too mad to be afraid, she ran toward him, throwing dirty sheets, clothes pins and even a wicker laundry basket. Quin didn’t need a second warning to know he was not welcome. Once again he was on the run. *That definitely wasn’t my perfect home, but I won’t give up,* he vowed.

In the distance, he noticed the roof of a peaked glass building shaped like a small barn. Quin was curious as he had never seen a barn made out of glass. He trotted forward

*After hiding out in the toolshed and escaping the police, Quin was ready for a little play time. He decided nothing could be more fun than shaking out sheets on a sunny day.*

with a friendly whinny, eager to meet the horses who he was certain lived in the barn. He looked around for pastures, but there was no fencing to be seen. Deciding the horses must be inside, he trotted up the gravel path that led to the glass barn.

He was puzzled by the strange barn. In all his years traveling the show circuit, he had never seen anything like it. When he looked through the glass walls, all he could see were green plants of different sizes and shapes. He nickered hello, but there wasn't any response from inside.

Not to be put off, he bumped the door open with his nose and walked in. To his great surprise, he didn't find a horse or even a stall. The only occupants of the glass barn were rows of potted, flowering plants that stood on long, wooden tables and hung from the ceiling.

Quin's nose curled at the strong smell of wet soil and fertilizer. He had never imagined a stable that housed only plants and dirt. On top of that, the air was far too hot and steamy for a horse to live comfortably. *This is definitely a very strange barn*, he mused. *Where are all the horses?*

Confused, Quin decided to snack on some of the plants while he tried to figure out who lived in the glass barn. He nibbled on some white flowers with long, curved petals. *This is the tastiest thing I've eaten since running away*, he decided, quickly gobbling up all the delicious blooms.

*Quin wasn't sure what the white flower was, but he knew it was the tastiest thing he had ever eaten.*

Finishing the last plant, he licked his lips just as a very angry man appeared in the doorway. Quin looked up with surprise, a white petal still dangling from his mouth.

The man's face was red with fury. "My prize flowers! You've eaten them all! They're ruined! What are you doing in my greenhouse?"

He grabbed a shovel from beside the door. Holding it over his head, he started toward Quin. "You'll pay for this, you horrible horse! It took me three years to develop those flowers and you've eaten them all up in minutes!"

The man was so angry that he didn't pay any attention to where he swung the shovel. Pots shattered and plants broke as he aimed for Quin, blocking his getaway through the door.

Frightened, Quin backed up quickly. In his rush, his haunches knocked into two potting benches. They fell over, crashing through the back side of the greenhouse. Glass flew in all directions as the benches smashed a big hole in the wall.

Quin didn't hesitate to take advantage of the unexpected escape route. He leapt through the hole to safety, barely dodging the last swing of the man's shovel. Chased away by his angry threats, he galloped back toward the safety of the woods positive that whatever lived in the glass barn was absolutely not horse friendly.

*That's definitely enough new home hunting for today*, Quin resolved, grateful to have escaped the wrath of yet another angry neighbor.

# Chapter Seven
# A Friend at Last

The sun was high overhead the next day before Quin worked up the courage to resume his search. This time he intended to thoroughly check out any prospective new home before attempting an introduction. His recent experiences had taught him that no matter how good a property looked, if the family didn't like or understand horses it could never be a home for him.

Quin trotted back toward the end of the neighborhood that he had yet to explore. He noticed a promising big yard surrounded by shade trees. Four women sat around a table on the back patio playing cards. *I think it's best to listen to what they have to say before I introduce myself,"* he decided, hiding behind a line of tall bushes at the back of the yard.

The woman facing his hiding place shuffled a deck of cards. “So, have you heard about the horse on the loose?”

The woman across the table looked up with surprise. “What loose horse, Marge?”

“Emily Hart swears a loose horse ran across her yard yesterday,” Marge answered. “He tore up their lawn with big hoof prints. Dick was furious!”

The third woman was doubtful. “That’s impossible. Whoever heard of a horse on the loose in the suburbs? There’s not even a stable nearby. Where would a horse come from?”

“I don’t know, but it’s the truth, Mindy,” the woman opposite assured her. “I heard he also got into George Andrews’ greenhouse. Made a total mess of it plus ruined those beautiful flowers he’s been raising for the garden show.”

Mindy nervously looked around the backyard. “Well, Carol, I certainly hope he’s not anywhere near here. I don’t mind watching horses from the other side of a big, strong fence, but the thought of a horse on the loose scares me. What would you do if he started to chase you?”

Carol laughed. “That’s total nonsense. Horses don’t chase people. They’re a lot more scared of us than we are of them. Besides, I think it might be fun to have a horse someday. I know the kids would love it.”

Quin peeked curiously around the bushes at the woman who said she wanted a horse. He liked her wide smile and friendly face. *Maybe, just maybe, she's the person I've been searching for*, he dared to hoped.

Marge began dealing cards from the deck. "Carol's absolutely right, Mindy. You don't have to worry about that horse. George Andrews and several other neighbors reported him to the police. I'm sure they've rounded up that troublesome creature by now and returned him to wherever he belongs."

Quin gave a worried snort at the mention of the police. *I'll have to work quickly if I'm going to find my new home before they catch up with me again. I doubt I'll be lucky to escape them a third time.*

Deciding it was worth taking a chance on Carol, Quin drew a hopeful breath and stepped around the bushes. Ears pricked with his friendliest expression, he started cautiously toward the patio. *It's now or never,* he resolved.

As Marge dealt the cards, she glanced up to see Quin slowly approaching. At the sight of him, she froze. The cards dropped from her hands to the ground, but she didn't notice. The closer Quin came, the wider her eyes grew with fear.

From across the table, Jean looked at her friend with concern. "Marge, what's wrong? Are you sick? You look like you've seen a ghost."

But Marge was too shocked to speak. Her lips kept mouthing the word *horse!* but no sound came out.

Puzzled, the other women turned to look where she was staring. “E-e-e-h!” they screamed in unison when they saw Quin less than ten feet away from the patio.

Jumping up, they ran for the safety of the house, knocking over their chairs as they fled. Even Carol who had said it might be fun to own a horse didn’t stop for a second look.

Only Marge didn’t move. She sat frozen in the same position still silently mouthing *horse!*

“Marge! Get in the house!” her friends screamed, huddled behind the safety of the back screen door. “Hurry before that horse hurts you!”

As Marge’s wide eyes met Quin’s, he didn’t realize she was frightened. Certain the woman hadn’t moved because she was waiting to meet him, he kept walking slowly forward, determined to convince her that he was friendly.

He stepped onto the patio beside her, nickering a soft greeting. When she still didn’t move, he stretched out his neck and gently nudged her shoulder with his nose. At his touch, Marge’s eyes rolled back in her head and she fainted, falling backwards off her chair.

“She’s hurt!” Jean screamed. “That horse hurt her! He pushed her over!”

*All Quin wanted to do was make a friend, but the woman at the card table was so frightened when he approached to make his introduction that she fainted.*

"Get away from Marge you terrible horse!" Mindy shrieked, gathering all her courage to run out of the house, threatening him with a pan. "Get away!"

"I didn't mean any harm," Quin nickered to reassure the women. "I just want to be friends." But when Mindy threw the pan which barely missed his head, he was convinced that it was a losing effort.

The angry women ran forward to save their friend who remained in a flat-out faint on the patio. They threw anything they could grab from the kitchen to scare Quin away. Deciding there were definitely no friends to be made at this house, he spun and galloped off.

Taking the quickest escape route, he jumped a hedge into the next yard. To his surprise, he nearly landed on top of a woman who lay sunning herself in a swim suit on a lounge chair. Her eyes were closed as she hummed along to a favorite song playing on her headphones.

Without room to swerve, Quin chipped in a short stride on landing and jumped the woman. Leaping high and wide, he tucked his hooves close to his chest to keep from hitting her.

"E-e-e-h!" she screamed, opening her eyes just in time to see Quin fly over her bare stomach.

The fear in her voice warned Quin that this was not the time to slow down or look back. He raced toward the hedge at the far side of her yard. Jumping it easily, he was soon out of earshot of the screaming woman.

Quin cantered on through the neighborhood until he was certain no one was chasing him. He finally came to a walk behind a red brick house with white shutters. A little girl with long brown braids sat cross-legged in the grass painting a picture.

He nickered a soft greeting without approaching. She looked up with a friendly smile. To his surprise, instead of running away or throwing something at him, she waved. He nickered again and her smile widened. It was the first smile anyone had shared with him since he began his journey to find a new home.

Quin started slowly forward, feeling drawn toward her. *Something about her smile reminds me of Dawn,* he realized, encouraged by the similarity.

The girl put down her brush but didn't get up or run away. Her smile only grew wider as she sat quietly waiting for him to reach her.

Quin stopped beside her, lowering his head until he could look directly in her eyes. Although his body towered above her, the little girl wasn't afraid. She reached out a tiny, trusting hand to pat his nose.

"Hi, horse," she cooed. "You sure are pretty. Where did you come from?"

*Quin's hopes rose that he had finally found his special person when he met the little girl who reminded him of Dawn.*

She pulled a handful of grass and offered it to him. He took it gently, careful not to nibble her little fingers. *Could she really be the one I've been looking for?* Quin dared to hope, enjoying her gentle touch against his muzzle.

Just when Quin started to believe he had finally found a friend, the door of the house swung open. "JILL!" a woman screamed in terror. "Don't be afraid. Mommy's coming! I'll save you from that awful horse!"

Quin lifted his head and pricked his ears towards her. "It's okay, we're buddies," he nickered to let the woman know that he meant no harm to her daughter.

But, the woman definitely misunderstood. "Don't you dare hurt my child!" she warned. "Back away, horse!"

Before Quin could respond, she whistled over her shoulder into the house. "Rex! Come here!"

A huge, black German shepherd quickly appeared at her side. "Get him, Rex! Get that horse!"

Without hesitating, Rex surged out of the house and across the backyard, barking fiercely.

Quin turned to flee, but he wasn't quick enough to escape Rex's sharp teeth nipping the back of his right leg. He kicked out, but the threat of a hoof wasn't enough to scare the dog away. Whichever way Quin swerved, Rex hung close.

"You might as well stop!" Rex growled, snapping at

Quin's heels. "You can't escape me!"

Quin galloped around the yard and down the road away from the house, but he couldn't lose the dog who was proving a very worthy opponent for an aging, road weary horse. *He might just be too much for me,* Quin thought fearfully. *No matter what I do, I can't shake him.*

As much as he wanted to stop and rest, he was certain that Rex would be on him with an angry fury unmatched by any of the others he had met on his journey. Quin had almost given up hope of escape when he saw a tall picket fence surrounding the next yard. Pushing his legs as fast as they would move, he galloped to the base of the fence. With a powerful thrust, he leapt up and over knowing it was his last chance.

To his relief, the fence proved too great a challenge for Rex to jump. While he angrily barked and clawed at the slats, Quin made his final escape of the day.

# Chapter Eight
# There's no Place Like Home

Without looking back, Quin galloped away from the neighborhood and the people who had made it very obvious there was no place in their lives for a horse. He didn't stop until he was too tired to take another stride. Exhausted, he licked at the painful bite wounds Rex had made to his legs. All hope of finding the perfect new home had been lost.

Discouraged, he realized the only option he had left was to return to his own stable. *Whatever Dawn has planned for me can't possibly be any worse than what I've been through since running away*, he decided. *Besides, I miss my stall and my stablemates.*

Admitting defeat, Quin put his head down and started walking. However, his journey had taken him so many miles that he was no longer certain which way led home. Hours passed as he circled and changed direction, hoping to see a familiar landmark. As much as he wanted to lie down and rest, he knew he had to keep moving even though every muscle in his body ached.

Clouds rolled in and the wind picked up. Sensing another storm was coming, he stumbled on as darkness fell. A rain drop plopped against his nose then a second hit between his ears. A moment later, it was pouring. Quin turned his head away from the storm. Ears drawn back, he kept walking, limping from the swelling in his legs.

Thunder rumbled overhead and the rain beat against Quin's back. He was cold and hungry, but still he kept on. The sight of a red barn in the distance wasn't even tempting. Although days before the lights would have looked like an inviting shelter against the storm, he stayed far away. Experience had taught him that whoever lived there would only chase him away.

Quin had almost given up hope of finding his way home when he came upon a large field. A flash of lightning revealed a single, tall oak tree standing in the center. He stopped, unable to believe his eyes. *Can that really be the tree where Dawn and I stopped so often for picnics on our rides?*

The sight of their special tree filled him with new hope.

*Wet, bruised and exhausted, Quin had almost given up hope of finding his way home when he came upon the tall oak tree where he and Dawn had often stopped for picnics on their rides.*

Suddenly, he didn't feel tired anymore. He threw back his head and whinnied into the wind with excitement as he galloped forward. The trail to the stable was now perfectly clear in his mind. With home so close, his weary legs found new energy to run on through the rain.

It was still dark when he finally cantered eagerly up the drive into his beloved stable yard. His hooves clicked against the gravel of the empty parking lot as he stopped in front of the barn. But when Quin tried to enter, he found all the doors closed tight against the storm.

"I'm home. Let me in!" he whinnied loudly, pawing at the door.

Finally, he heard footsteps from inside, hurrying in his direction. A moment later the door swung open and Quin found himself face-to-face with Andy. After so many days of being turned away by angry humans, the genuine love and concern on his friend's face filled Quin's heart to overflowing.

The startled groom rubbed the sleep from his eyes. "Quin! Is it really you? Where have you been, old man?"

For once the nickname didn't bother Quin as he happily nuzzled his friend. He sniffed his pockets searching for the sugar that he was certain would be there. Andy immediately rewarded him with two cubes and a big neck hug.

For the first time since running away, Quin felt safe and loved. "I'm home. I'm finally home!" he nickered with joy.

Andy was concerned as he gently ran his hands over Quin's scratched body and swollen legs. "What happened to you, boy? How did you get so cut up? Some of these look like bites! Seems like you've had a real rough time of it. Whatever made you run off like that? We've all been worried sick."

He went back into the barn with Quin limping at his side. "Let's get you settled in your stall. Then I'll get the vet right out to take a look at you. After all you've been through, we need to get you checked out."

Quin didn't need help finding his old stall. The door was open when he reached it, but he paused before entering. He stuck his head in and looked around. The floor was covered with clean, fresh shavings. Sweet smelling, green hay filled the manger and a full bucket of fresh water hung from the wall. It looked so welcoming as though it had been waiting for his return.

*It's just like I left it,* Quin thought happily as he stepped through the door. In that moment, his suspicions were put to rest as it was obvious that no other horse had been brought in to take his place.

His stablemate nickered a friendly welcome, but Quin was too tired to do more than touch the chestnut gelding's nose through the stall bars in greeting. He knew there would be lots of time in the morning to share his adventures as he sank gratefully down into the soft bed of shavings. He was so exhausted that even the hay and water couldn't tempt him to stay awake.

Andy crouched down on the ground beside him. He lovingly used a thick towel to dry his soaked coat. He stroked Quin's neck as he picked some of the briars out of his tangled mane. "Take it easy, my friend. The vet will be here real soon to fix you up. A little rest and some good food will make you feel good as new. Now get some sleep."

Quin didn't need any encouragement. With a contented sigh, he rolled out flat. As soon as he shut his eyes, he fell into a deep, peaceful sleep. For the first time since running away, he didn't have any nightmares of police chases or yelling neighbors.

He only half awoke when the vet arrived. The doctor gave him a thorough exam then rubbed medicine into the bites and cuts on his legs. When he was satisfied that all the injuries were minor, he gave Quin a shot that stopped the pain and made him fall into a deeper sleep.

The next morning Quin was startled awake by the sound of feet running down the concrete barn aisle toward his stall. Still groggy from the vet's shot, at first he couldn't remember where he was. After the stress of the past few days, he was overtaken by fear. Sensing the need to run from the approaching footsteps, he started to scramble to his feet.

But then a voice that he knew and loved better than any other shouted down the aisle. "QUIN!" In that moment, he gratefully sank back into the shavings knowing he was safe as that voice and those footsteps running toward him belonged to Dawn.

She rushed into the stall and knelt down beside him. "Oh, Quin," she cried, hugging his neck to her chest. "What happened? Why did you run away? Where have you been? I was so scared I'd never see you again. I came home from school as soon as Mom and Dad told me you were gone."

She cradled his head, stroking his forelock. "Everyone was so worried. The police kept calling to say they had found you, but when we'd get there with the trailer, you had disappeared again. Day and night all our friends from the barn have been out looking for you."

Quin sighed, nuzzling her hand as he took the carrots she offered. With Dawn beside him, his legs didn't hurt as much and he didn't feel tired anymore.

She gently ran her fingers along his neck, tugging on his mane with the special touch that he loved. "What would I do without you, Quin? Another horse could never replace you. We've shared so many things and you've taught me so much. I could never part with you. There's not enough money in the world to buy you. You've worked so hard for so many

*Quin snuggled his head against Dawn with a sigh of happiness, realizing his difficult journey had led him full circle back to the perfect home.*

years that you've earned a real rest, but not in a stall here at the stable."

Quin pulled his head away, suddenly feeling uneasy as he looked at her. *What does she mean, not here? Where else would I live?*

"You ran away before I had a chance to share our plans," Dawn continued, gently running her hand down his blaze. "Dad just bought a new home in the country. We're going to move there as soon as I get out of school this summer."

Her smile widened as she described it. "The property is wonderful, but the best part is there's a beautiful barn and pasture just perfect for you. So, when we move, you're coming with us. It'll be your forever home.

"You're going to be a real country gentleman," she promised, wiping away the tears that still ran down her cheeks. "The people next door have horses too, so you'll have plenty of company. And, there are even miles and miles of trails just waiting for us to explore."

Quin couldn't believe his ears. All the time he had wasted worrying that Dawn no longer cared and wanted to sell him, she had really been planning to share her special new home with him. He suddenly realized that it had taken running away to discover that the perfect home was the one he already had. Quin nuzzled her shoulder then threw back his head with a loud, joyous whinny, knowing Dawn would understand.

# Author Biography

Leslie McDonald grew up in Chicago, Illinois and attended DePauw University. She is the author of *Down the Aisle, Musings of a Horse Farm Corgi, Journeys with Horses, Making Magic* and *Tic-Tac*. A Grand Prix level dressage trainer with over 50 professional years in the industry, she lives on a horse farm in southern Ohio where she happily teaches lessons and writes books about the special people and animals who have blessed her life.

Visit www.fcfarm.com for more information and to connect with Leslie.

Made in the USA
Monee, IL
13 October 2022

6037ba81-049d-4b3b-abea-891ec3e9e389R01